101 DALMATIANS

This special edition was printed for Kohl's Department Stores, Inc. (for distribution on behalf of Kohl's Cares, LLC, its wholly owned subsidiary), by Disney Press, New York/Los Angeles.

Kohl's
1204201-00
123387
07/14–08/14

Printed in China
First Edition
1 3 5 7 9 10 8 6 4 2
ISBN 978-1-4847-2157-5
G615-7693-2-14182

For more Disney Press fun, visit www.disneybooks.com

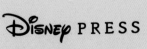

New York • Los Angeles

My name's Pongo. My story begins in London. I lived in a flat with my pet, Roger Radcliffe. Roger was struggling to write the perfect love song. A love song! What did Roger know about love? I decided to help Roger find a wife. He needed someone to love, and, frankly, so did I.

One sunny day, I saw the most beautiful creature on four legs. She had a straight, pointed tail, and the most magnificent spots! And the woman behind her was lovely as well! I knew I'd never find another pair like that. So I grabbed my leash and ran to the front door. I began to bark.

As soon as Roger opened the door, I yanked him down the sidewalk and toward the park.

I was determined for Roger and the woman to meet! When we reached the park, I dragged Roger after her, then wrapped my leash around their legs. Before I knew it, the two stumbled . . . right into the pond!

Suddenly, the woman began to laugh. So did Roger. That's when I glanced at the four-legged creature. To my surprise, she smiled!

That was our lucky day. The next spring we were married, Roger and Anita, Perdita and I.

One afternoon, Perdita told me that our lives were about to change. She was having puppies.

I couldn't believe it. I was going to be a dad!

Time passed, and soon Perdita gave birth. We had not four, not five, but fifteen puppies! Then one night a strange creature showed up at our happy home: Cruella De Vil. Cruella was one of Anita's schoolmates, and she wanted our puppies!

"I'll take them all," Cruella said. "The whole litter. Just name your price."

Roger crossed his arms. "Never," he said. "The puppies will never leave this house."

Furious, Cruella stomped around the room. "All right, keep the little beasts," she screeched. "But I warn you, I'll get even. You fools."

The little ones brought us nothing but joy.

One night, Perdy and I went for a walk with Roger and Anita. We left the puppies home with Nanny. She had just put them to bed when the doorbell rang. On the porch stood a tall, skinny man and a shorter, fatter fellow.

Nanny tried to shut the door, but the tall one pushed against it and burst into the house.

The two men locked Nanny in a bedroom. By the time she escaped, our puppies were missing!

I knew I needed to do something. The next night when Anita and Roger took us for our walk, I decided to try the Twilight Bark. It was the fastest way to send news. If our puppies were anywhere in the city, the London dogs would know.

Soon the sound of howling dogs echoed across the city. Finally, the Twilight Bark reached the country. A cat named Sergeant Tibs heard it and woke his friend, an old English sheepdog named the Colonel.

"An alert?" the Colonel yelped. He listened closely until finally he understood. Fifteen Dalmatian puppies were missing.

Tibs jumped up. He had heard puppies at Cruella De Vil's old place two days earlier!

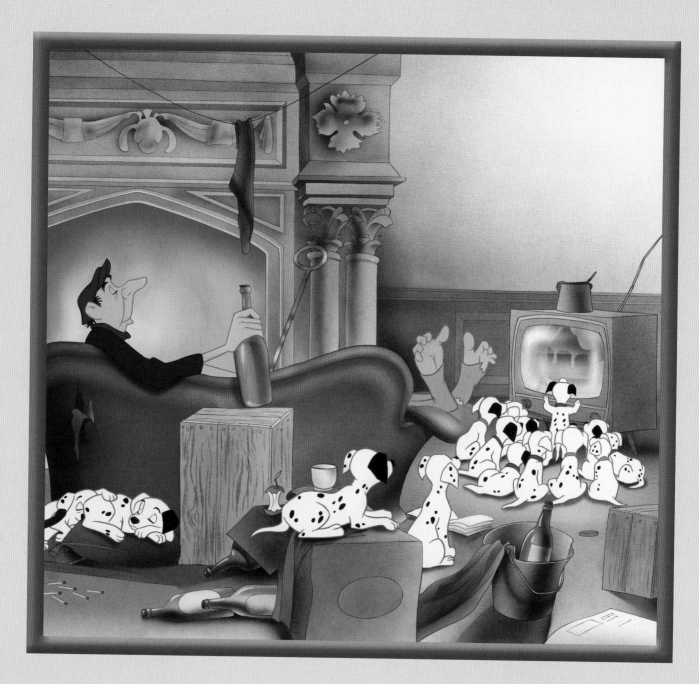

The Colonel raised a brow. "Puppies at the old De Vil place? Strange. No one's lived there for years. Hmmm. We'd better investigate."

At the mansion, light seeped through a small hole in the wall. Tibs squeezed through it and saw a room full of Dalmatian puppies!

As Tibs watched the puppies, he heard two men talking. Cruella wanted to use our puppies' fur to make a coat!

While Tibs helped the puppies escape, the London dogs used the Twilight Bark to give us directions to the old De Vil place.

The skinny man had just noticed that the puppies were missing when we arrived. Growling, Perdita and I crashed through the window. We would distract the scoundrels while Tibs led the puppies to safety.

We managed to get out of the place in one piece, but our trouble was far from over. We hadn't rescued just our fifteen pups, but ninety-nine puppies in all! Perdita and I knew we had to keep them all safe.

"We'll take them all home with us," I said. "Somehow."

Perdita and I guided the puppies toward London, trying to make sure no one got lost. But the snow made it impossible to cover our tracks, and we worried we would be found.

It wasn't long before the puppies were exhausted. Luckily, a collie came running toward us.

"Pongo," he cried.

Surprised to hear my name, I looked up. It seemed everyone had been listening to the Twilight Bark.

"We'd almost given up hope," the collie continued. "We have shelter for you at the farm across the road."

What luck! A little later we found ourselves inside a warm and cozy barn. The puppies were terribly hungry, but we had nothing to feed them.

"Perhaps the little ones would like a little warm milk?" one of the cows asked. "It's fresh."

"Milk!" the puppies yelped, and gathered around. Perdy and I hardly knew how to thank the cows.

The next morning we continued our journey through the snowy countryside. We hadn't gone far before we were met by a Labrador. He had found a furniture van we could ride home in.

Just then I saw Cruella's car coming down the road. We quickly hid in a blacksmith's shop.

As Cruella's car passed, I looked at the puppies. Some of them were covered in soot from the fireplace. Then it hit me. . . .

"Everybody roll in the soot!" I cried. "We're all going to be Labradors!"

Giggling, the puppies rolled in the soot. Cruella would be looking for our spots. She'd never recognize us without them!

The trick worked! No one paid any attention when I began loading the puppies into the van.

As I helped the last few pups, a clump of snow fell on Lucky, burying him. I quickly pulled him out with my teeth, but the snow had washed him clean. Our cover had been blown.

As the van started, I tossed Lucky up to Perdita and leaped up on the back myself. But Cruella was right on our tail.

Cruella raced after us, trying to force the van off the road.

"Hey, lady!" shouted the driver desperately. "What are you doing?" But Cruella just continued to ram the side of the van.

Suddenly, Cruella lost control of her car. She crashed through the barricade and bounded down into a snowbank. She wouldn't be chasing us anymore!

Tired and dirty, we made our way home. I was greeting Nanny when I heard Anita cry, "Who are all these strange dogs?"

I had forgotten that our coats were still black! But Nanny had noticed the paw marks I had made on her white apron. "They're just covered with soot!" she shouted.

Roger pulled out his handkerchief and wiped my face. "Pongo! Is that you?" he said, grinning.

Nanny grabbed a broom and began sweeping soot off the puppies. "This is Patch, and Rolly, and here's Penny! My dear, they're all here." Puzzled, she gazed around the room. "And, hmmm, there's a whole lot more!"

Anita and Roger began counting. Imagine their surprise when they reached a total of one hundred and one Dalmatians!

"What will we do with them?" Anita asked.

"We'll keep them!" Roger said. "We'll buy a big place in the country, and we'll have a plantation! A Dalmatian plantation."

Roger hurried over to the piano. He had written a song while Perdita and I had been out searching for our puppies. I knew he had written his first big hit. Maybe we really *would* get a Dalmatian plantation. One thing was certain: Roger and I would never be lonely again.

• • • • • • • • • •